THE CANTERBURY TALES:
CHANTICLEER

Retold by Margaret Berrill
Illustrated by Jane Bottomley

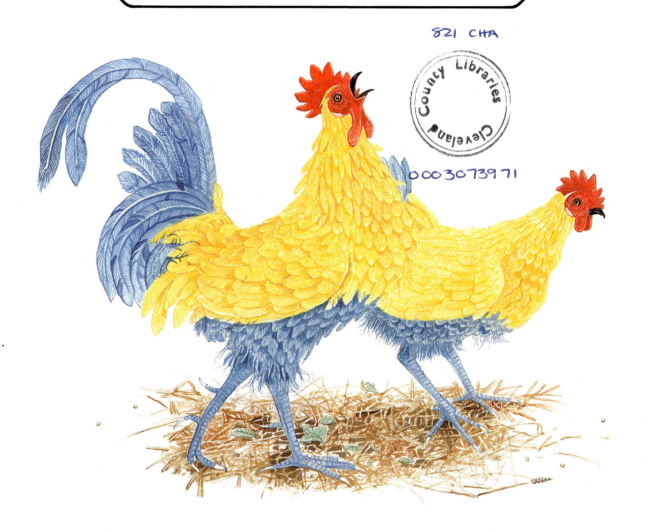

Methuen Children's Books
in association with Belitha Press Ltd.

Note: The story of a vain cock who is tricked by a sly fox occurs in many languages. The most famous English version is the tale told by the Nun's Priest in Geoffrey Chaucer's *Canterbury Tales*. These were written five hundred years ago in the language, now called 'Middle English', from which our own modern English developed.

MB

Copyright © in this format Belitha Press Ltd, 1986
Text copyright © Margaret Berrill 1986
Illustrations copyright © Jane Bottomley 1986
Art Director: Treld Bicknell
First published in Great Britain in 1986
by Methuen Children's Books Ltd,
11 New Fetter Lane, London EC4P 4EE
Conceived, designed and produced by Belitha Press Ltd,
31 Newington Green, London N16 9PU
ISBN 0 416 63990 9 (hardback)
ISBN 0 416 96210 6 (paperback)
Printed in Hong Kong by South China Printing Co.

ONE SPRING EVENING FIVE HUNDRED YEARS AGO
a large group of travellers met at the Tabard inn,
near London, on their way to Canterbury.
They were pilgrims, going there
to visit the grave of a holy man.
To help pass the time on their journey
they agreed to take turns at telling stories.
The innkeeper would travel with them
to judge whose tale was best
and the prize would be a free dinner.
Amongst the travellers was a wise and kindly priest
and when it came to his turn,
this is the tale he told.

'ONCE, LONG AGO, THERE WAS A POOR OLD WIDOW
who lived in a small cottage in a valley
beside a clump of trees.
With her two daughters she lived a quiet life
for she had not much money or land,
just enough to keep three pigs, three cows and a sheep called Molly.
The widow could not afford rich food,
so she was never ill from overeating.
She had milk and brown bread, bacon,
and sometimes an egg or two which her own hens laid.

OUTSIDE HER COTTAGE WAS A YARD
surrounded by a fence and a ditch,
and there she kept a cock called Chanticleer.
No other cock could equal his crowing.
His voice was sweeter than the church organ
and he told the time better than any clock.
He knew by instinct how the minutes passed
and crew at every hour.
This fine cock had seven pretty hens
to keep him company.
The loveliest of all was Pertelote.
She was so smart and friendly
and had such dainty manners
that Chanticleer had loved her
since she was one week old.

EARLY ONE MORNING CHANTICLEER
sat among the hens next to Pertelote
on the rafters in the kitchen.
He started to moan
as though he was having a bad dream.
Pertelote was terrified and cried,
"Whatever is the matter, my love?
Why are you moaning?"
"Don't be afraid," said Chanticleer,
"but I've had such a terrible dream
that my heart is still thudding."

"I pray to God to keep us all safe,
for this dream is a warning.
This is what I dreamt.
As I was roaming up and down in our yard
I saw a creature like a dog
which would have pounced on me and killed me!
His coat was yellowish red with black-tipped ears and tail,
he had a small snout and glowing eyes . . .
I still feel almost dead with fright!"

"Afraid?" cried Pertelote.
"You should be ashamed of yourself!
Do you expect me to love a coward?
Are you scared of a dream
when everyone knows from the wisest teachers
that dreams are all nonsense?
I'll tell you the cause of your dream –
it's overeating! I will soon cure you.
You must eat nothing but worms for a couple of days
then take my medicine for an upset stomach.
Now cheer up, and don't be afraid of a silly old dream!"
"You say," replied Chanticleer,
"that the wisest teachers tell us
that dreams are nonsense.
But I have read many books which disagree.
Let me tell you just one story I have read."

"IN THIS STORY THERE WERE TWO MEN
who wanted to cross the sea to a far country.
The night before they planned to sail,
one of them dreamt
that a man stood by his bed and told him
that if he sailed next day
he would surely be drowned.
When day came he begged his friend not to sail
for fear that the dream would come true.
His friend jeered at him,
and said that he would still go.
Before he was halfway across the sea
there was an accident, and ship and man sank together."

"So you see, dear Pertelote," Chanticleer went on,
"that no one should ignore warnings in dreams.
And please don't mention medicine –
you know I hate the stuff!
Now let's drop the subject, for when I see your lovely face
and the red rings round your eyes,
I forget all about dreams."

WITH THIS, CHANTICLEER FLEW DOWN FROM THE RAFTERS
for day had now come. All his hens followed him.
He clucked to show them a grain of corn
lying in the yard.
He looked like a royal prince
strutting proudly up and down, or like a fierce lion
with his toes scarcely touching the ground.
He found another grain of corn and when he clucked
all the hens came running up.

CHANTICLEER LOOKED UP AT THE SUN
and knew that it was nine o'clock.
He crowed cheerfully and said to Pertelote,
"What a lovely day it is.
Listen to the birds
and look at all the lovely flowers.
I feel very happy today."
But he was not to be happy for long.
During the night a wicked, sly fox,
who for three years had lived nearby
in the clump of trees,
had broken through the fence
into Chanticleer's yard.
The fox lay crouching in a bed of cabbages until midday
waiting for a chance to pounce on Chanticleer.

PERTELOTE WAS ENJOYING A DUSTBATH IN THE SAND
while all the other hens sunned themselves nearby.
Chanticleer was singing away gaily
when his eye fell upon a butterfly among the cabbages.
Suddenly he noticed the fox crouching there.
"Cok, Cok!" he shrieked,
and would have fled in terror.

But before he could move, the fox quickly said,
"Oh sir! Where are you off to?
Don't be afraid of me! I'm your friend!
Surely you don't think that I would hurt you?
I only came here to listen to you sing.
Your voice is like an angel's;
it reminds me of your father's,
and he was my favourite singer.
Your father and mother used to visit me in my house.
When he sang, he would concentrate hard,
his eyes shut tight, standing on tiptoe
with his neck stretched out.
Won't you do me a great favour,
and sing for me like your father?"

CHANTICLEER BEGAN TO FLAP HIS WINGS.
He was so flattered
that he did not suspect a trick.
He stood on tiptoe with his neck stretched out,
his eyes shut tight,
and began to crow as loud as he could.
In a flash the fox leapt up,
seized Chanticleer by the throat
and carried him off on his back towards the trees.

When they saw Chanticleer being carried off
the hens set up such a screeching
that the widow and her daughters
ran out of the cottage.
They were just in time to see
the fox make for the woods
with the cock on his back.

"HELP, HELP! STOP THIEF! A FOX!"
they cried, and ran after him
followed by a crowd of men with big sticks,
the dog, the maid, cows, calves and even the pigs
running fit to burst, terrified by the noise.

The ducks squawked, the geese flew up over the trees
and even the bees swarmed out of their hive.
Never was such a noise heard before
as when the crowd chased after the fox,
blowing and hooting
on trumpets of brass and wood and bone and horn –
it seemed as though the skies would fall.

NOW SEE HOW CHANTICLEER'S LUCK CHANGED.
Although he was terrified,
slung over the fox's back,
he managed to speak and said,
"Sir! If I were you I'd shout,
'Run home you country bumpkins!
Now that I've reached the edge of the wood
I'm going to keep this cock whatever you do
and eat him up right away!' "
The fox replied, "I'll do just that,"
but as he spoke,
Chanticleer suddenly leapt out of his mouth
and flew high up on a tree.

W HEN THE FOX SAW THAT THE COCK HAD GONE
he cried, "Oh dear, Chanticleer!
I must have scared you
when I snatched you out of the yard.
But believe me, I wouldn't hurt you.
Come down and I'll tell you
what I meant to do!"

"Oh no," replied the cock,
"I would be a fool
to let you trick me more than once.
I won't be flattered into singing again
with my eyes shut.
Never shut your eyes
when they ought to stay open."
"And what's more," replied the fox,
" never open your mouth
when you ought to keep it shut."

AND SO IT WAS THAT DAY
that the cock and the fox taught each other a lesson,'
the priest said as he finished his tale.
The innkeeper thanked the priest
and looked around at the travellers
to see whose tale should be told next
on the road to Canterbury.